Trains

Illustrated by Roger Stewart

OXFORD
UNIVERSITY PRESS

This book belongs to

OXFORD
UNIVERSITY PRESS

Great Clarendon Street, Oxford OX2 6DP

Oxford University Press is a department of the University of Oxford.
It furthers the University's objective of excellence in research, scholarship,
and education by publishing worldwide in

Oxford New York

Athens Auckland Bangkok Bogotá Buenos Aires Calcutta
Cape Town Chennai Dar es Salaam Delhi Florence Hong Kong Istanbul
Karachi Kuala Lumpur Madrid Melbourne Mexico City Mumbai
Nairobi Paris São Paulo Singapore Taipei Tokyo Toronto Warsaw

with associated companies in Berlin Ibadan

Oxford is a registered trade mark of Oxford University Press
in the UK and in certain other countries

Text copyright © Dennis Hamley 2001
Illustrations copyright © Roger Stewart 2001

The moral rights of the author and artist have been asserted

First published 2001

Hardback ISBN 0–19–910653-3
Paperback ISBN 0–19–910654–1

1 3 5 7 9 10 8 6 4 2

Printed in Edelvives, Spain.

Contents

▶ Once long ago

Many years ago, a boy watched the trains.

He loved the steam engines. They were huge. Smoke and steam poured out of their chimneys. They made deafening noises. They smelt of oil and smoke.

When the boy went by train to the seaside, it was the greatest adventure of his year. He hoped the railways would never change.

Great Western
Cornish Riviera Express

▶ Now

Now that boy is a man. He still watches the trains. They are sleek and fast.

They don't belch out smoke.

Yes, the steam engines are gone.

Eurostar

The first railways

Two hundred years ago, there were no trains. If you didn't have a horse, you walked.

At that time there was an engineer and inventor called James Watt. One day he was watching a kettle boiling water. He noticed how the steam rose and pushed the lid up.

He wondered why.

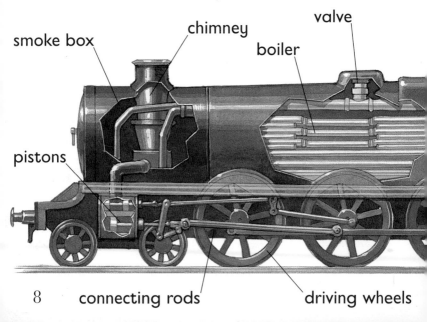

smoke box

chimney

valve

boiler

pistons

8   connecting rods

driving wheels

The answer is – steam makes pressure. That's what pushed the kettle lid up.

James Watt thought this pressure might be a force to make steam engines to pump water out of coal mines, tin mines and quarries. He was right.

This is how steam engines work.

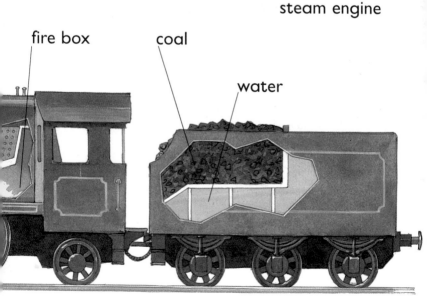

steam engine

fire box

coal

water

Then a man called Richard Trevithick wondered if, instead of horses, steam engines could pull loaded trucks. He made a steam engine which would run on rails.

Some people thought it was a toy.

Others said, "It's not a toy. We could build a big railway to carry goods and people."

Trevithick's "Catch-me-who-can" engine

Stephenson's "Locomotion" built in 1825

An engineer called George Stephenson built the first public railway from Stockton to Darlington in England. It opened in 1825. The Stockton and Darlington Railway was only a few miles long. People wondered if railways could cover long distances.

▶ The main line

George Stephenson built the first long distance railway. It went from Liverpool to Manchester.

There were valleys to cross and hills to climb. There were marshes where the land was soft. The rails would sink. So would the trains.

People said he'd never finish it. But he did.

The railway opened in 1830. But something sad happened on the very first day. It was the first train accident. Mr Huskisson, Member of Parliament, was run over and killed.

Olive Mount cutting on the Liverpool and Manchester Railway

Some people were frightened by the accident. Others were frightened because the trains travelled so fast. Twenty miles an hour! Before this, nothing could go faster than a horse.

Did you know...
There was a competition to find the best steam engine. George Stephenson won it with his engine "Rocket". "Rocket" was the first engine to run on a main line railway.

Stephenson's
"Rocket"

▶ Building the railways

Pilatusbahn in Switzerland

It's not easy to build a railway which goes a long way. For a start, ordinary steam engines can't climb mountains. The few which can have special wheels and rails with teeth. They go very slowly.

For ordinary trains, there would have to be bridges over rivers, tunnels and cuttings through hills and embankments over valleys.

Who did all the work to build the railways? Thousands of men with shovels, spades and barrows. They were called "navvies".

Wherever the navvies went, they changed the land for ever, across Europe, America, India, Russia and China.

Building railways was dangerous work. Earth could slip and rocks could fall in cuttings and tunnels. There could be sudden floods. Many navvies were killed.

0-6-2 tender engine in India

But once the railways were finished, what changes they made! People became used to trains. Nobody was frightened of them any more.

Did you know...
"Navvy" is short for "navigator". A navigator is someone who finds the way.

▶ The best years of the railways

For one hundred years, railways were the only way to travel across land quickly. They covered huge distances, across America, Canada, India and Russia.

The Trans-Siberian Express ran from Vladivostok in the east of Russia to Moscow in the west. That's halfway around the world. The journey lasted two weeks. The train became the passengers' home.

Trains got better and better.

People said nothing could ever replace railways. But things changed.

Trans-Siberian Express

▶ Changes

The petrol engine was invented. In the 1890s the first cars came on to the roads. Orville and Wilbur Wright flew the first aeroplane in 1903.

Time passed. Many people bought cars. Bus fares were cheap. Aeroplanes were big, safe and fast.

Who wanted to travel on smoky old trains?

Stanier "Black Five"

Volkswagen Beetle   Routemaster

The steam engines were scrapped.
New engines were built which were
cleaner and faster.

Now in most countries, there are
no steam engines left, except in
museums or on preserved railways.

The new trains

Many new trains are powered by diesel engines. Here is a diesel train. It is called the Inter-City 125. It was built more than twenty-five years ago.

Inter-City 125

It still runs all over the railways of Britain. It can travel at 125 miles, or 200 kilometres, an hour.

Other trains are powered by electricity. Here are two electric trains. One is the TGV, the "High Speed Train". It runs in France.

TGV

Bullet Train

The other is the Bullet Train, from Japan.

But trains are always being made better. New trains will be built which will go even faster and more smoothly. One day they may not even touch the rails but float on a cushion of air!

Maglev

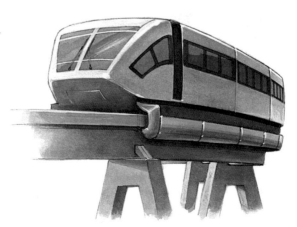

25

That boy who watched the steam trains long ago would hardly recognise them. But without the steam engines which ruled the railways for one hundred and fifty years there would be no railways now.

▶ Superstar steam engines

Steam engines could be big, small, fast or slow. Here is the biggest.

In America, the Union Pacific Railroad built the biggest engine in the world. It was called "Big Boy". "Big Boy" had sixteen driving wheels. It hauled huge freight trains across the United States. Though it was forty metres long, it could go round sharp bends.

"Big boy"

Here is the fastest steam engine ever made.

Sixty years ago, a man called Nigel Gresley built some streamlined steam engines. They were painted blue.

One day in 1938, one engine called "Mallard" ran faster than any engine had before. It went at 126 miles, or 203 kilometres, an hour. No steam engine will go so fast again.

An engine just like "Mallard", but named "Sir Nigel Gresley" after the man who built it, still hauls special trains.

There is a big Railway Museum in York. You can see "Mallard" there.

"Mallard"

MALLARD

Nº 4468

◢ Glossary

This glossary will help you to understand what some important words mean. You can find them in this book by using the page numbers given below.

cutting A cutting is a way cut through steep hills because trains cannot go over them. If the hill is too high, a tunnel is bored through it instead. **12,16**

diesel A diesel engine uses oil for fuel. Lorries, buses and some cars as well as railway engines have diesel engines. **22**

driving wheels The biggest wheels on a steam engine are called the driving wheels. They make the engine move along the rails. **27**

embankment When the railway crosses a valley, a bank is built to keep the rails level. This is called an embankment. If the valley is very wide, a long bridge called a viaduct may be built instead. **16**

engineer The person who built railway engines and made railways, bridges and many other things was called an engineer. In the United States engine drivers are called engineers. **8, 11**

main line The main line is a long railway between big cities on which fast trains run. Shorter lines are called "branch lines". **12**

railroad/railway In the United States and Canada railways are called railroads.

Reading Together

Oxford Reds have been written by leading children's authors who have a passion for particular non-fiction subjects. So as well as up-to-date information, fascinating facts and stunning pictures, these books provide powerful writing which draws the reader into the text.

Oxford Reds are written in simple language, checked by educational advisors. There is plenty of repetition of words and phrases, and all technical words are explained. They are an ideal vehicle for helping your child develop a love of reading – by building fluency, confidence and enjoyment.

You can help your child by reading the first few pages out loud, then encourage him or her to continue alone. You could share the reading by taking turns to read a page or two. Or you could read the whole book aloud, so your child knows it well before tackling it alone.

Oxford Reds will help your child develop a love of reading and a lasting curiosity about the world we live in.

Sue Palmer
Writer and Literacy Consultant